ROUND

Written by Joyce Sidman *Illustrated by* Taeeun Yoo

Houghton Mifflin Harcourt
Boston New York

For family and friends whose love encircles us in times of need.
—J.S.

To my family, with love
—T.Y.

www.hmhco.com

The illustrations in this book are mixed media with printed texture.
The text type was set in Bryant.

Library of Congress Cataloging-in-Publication Data
Names: Sidman, Joyce, author. | Yoo, Taeeun, illustrator.
Title: Round / Joyce Sidman ; [illustrated by] Taeeun Yoo.
Description: Boston ; New York : Houghton Mifflin Harcourt, [2017] |
Audience: Ages 4–7. | Audience: K to grade 3.
Identifiers: LCCN 2016014695 | ISBN 9780544387614 (hardcover)
Subjects: LCSH: Shapes—Juvenile literature. | Geometry,
Solid—Juvenile literature.
Classification: LCC QA445.5 .S537 2017 | DDC 516.15—dc23
LC record available at https://lccn.loc.gov/2016014695

Manufactured in China
SCP 10 9 8 7 6 5 4 3 2 1
4500631751

I love round things.

I like to feel their smoothness.

My hands want to reach
around their curves.

I love to see round things grow.

Some start out round . . .

like a seed

or an egg,
waiting to hatch.

Some swell into roundness:

budding,

ripening,

stretching

toward the sun.

Some are a different shape
to begin with,

but slowly, over time,

all the sharp edges wear off.

I love to watch round things move.
They are so good at it!

Rolling,

spinning,

bouncing.

I always wonder where they're headed.

I love round things when they're hidden
and you have to discover them.

Some hold secrets inside.
Some are almost too tiny to see.

I love how water can be round,
gathered in beads of silver . . .
or falling in wet splats,
leaving circles of ripples behind.

I love when round things
pop up quickly . . .
and last only a moment.

Or spin together

slowly . . .

and lost billions of years.

Or show themselves,
night after night,
rounder and rounder,
until the whole sky holds its breath.

I can be round, too . . .
in a circle of friends
with no one left out.

Or, I can curl by myself
in a warm, round ball.

I love round things.

Why are so many things in nature round?

Round is cozy. Round nests and burrows are comfortable—no sharp edges. When we curl up in a ball, either alone or together, we feel warm and protected. Sharp pieces of grit inside oyster shells become round pearls over time because the oyster adds layers to make them smoother. Pebbles wear down to roundness through the tumbling movement of waves on a sandy shore.

Round is sturdy. A round egg or seed distributes weight evenly over its entire shell, minimizing stress on any one point, to help bear the body of a parent bird, or the crush of an animal's digestive system.

Round spreads out. Trees often form spheres (three-dimensional circles) as their branches grow toward sunlight in all directions equally. Mushrooms open like umbrellas to scatter their spores. Drops hitting water radiate circular ripples from a central point.

Round rolls! Round nuts, fruits, and seeds roll well, allowing them to scatter — and grow new plants — more easily. Likewise, dung beetles form dung into round balls in order to roll them to their burrows.

Round is balanced. Spheres hold the most volume with the least amount of surface area. Thus, bubbles and water droplets naturally form spheres as their surface tension contains the force of the air or water inside them. Planets are round because gravity pulls equally from the planet's central core to every point on its outer surface.

Round is beautiful. So many round things are important to us: the faces and eyes we seek out. The food we eat. The sun and moon that measure our days. The hugs that hold us tight. Round things are snug, symmetrical, cosmic. They remind us of our interconnectedness, and represent the cycle of seasons and of life. They bring us back to where we started. That is why I love them.

Joyce Sidman